# PARADISE TRADING
[

## Website: www.kulsoo

GW00383956

# INVOICE

TO: _____     DATE: _____

_____

| ITEM | QTY | PRICE | TOTAL |
|------|-----|-------|-------|
|      |     |       |       |
|      |     |       |       |
|      |     |       |       |
|      |     |       |       |
|      |     |       |       |
|      |     |       |       |
|      |     |       |       |

TOTAL

Registered Company of UK & EU.@
Trademarked @
Product tested Certified@
Council Approved@

## THANK YOU!

114 Bizspace Limited, Business Park, Kings Road, Tyseley, Birmingham, B112AL

PHONE NUMBER:
+44 7878068906

RECEIPT

# RECEIPT

# RECEIPT

# INVOICE

TO: _____    DATE: _____

_____

| ITEM | QTY | PRICE | TOTAL |
|------|-----|-------|-------|
|      |     |       |       |
|      |     |       |       |
|      |     |       |       |
|      |     |       |       |
|      |     |       |       |
|      |     |       |       |
|      |     |       |       |

**TOTAL**

Registered Company of UK & EU.@
Trademarked @
Product tested Certified@
Council Approved@

# THANK YOU!

114 Bizspace Limited, Business Park, Kings Road, Tyseley, Birmingham, B112AL

PHONE NUMBER:
+44 7878068906

RECEIPT

RECEIPT

# RECEIPT

# INVOICE

TO: _____    DATE: _____

_____

| ITEM | QTY | PRICE | TOTAL |
|------|-----|-------|-------|
|  |  |  |  |
|  |  |  |  |
|  |  |  |  |
|  |  |  |  |
|  |  |  |  |

TOTAL

Registered Company of UK & EU.@
Trademarked @
Product tested Certified@
Council Approved@

## THANK YOU!

114 Bizspace Limited, Business Park, Kings Road, Tyseley, Birmingham, B112AL

PHONE NUMBER:
+44 7878068906

RECEIPT

# RECEIPT

RECEIPT

# PARADISE TRADING LTD (BIRMINGHAM)

Website: www.kulsoomtrading.com

# INVOICE

TO: _____    DATE: _____

_____

| ITEM | QTY | PRICE | TOTAL |
|------|-----|-------|-------|
|      |     |       |       |
|      |     |       |       |
|      |     |       |       |
|      |     |       |       |
|      |     |       |       |
|      |     |       |       |
|      |     |       |       |

TOTAL

Registered Company of UK & EU.@
Trademarked @
Product tested Certified@
Council Approved@

# THANK YOU!

114 Bizspace Limited, Business Park, Kings Road, Tyseley, Birmingham, B112AL

PHONE NUMBER:
+44 7878068906

# RECEIPT

RECEIPT

# RECEIPT

# INVOICE

TO: _____    DATE: _____

_____

| ITEM | QTY | PRICE | TOTAL |
|------|-----|-------|-------|
|  |  |  |  |
|  |  |  |  |
|  |  |  |  |
|  |  |  |  |
|  |  |  |  |
|  |  |  |  |
|  |  |  |  |
|  |  |  |  |

TOTAL

Registered Company of UK & EU.@
Trademarked @
Product tested Certified@
Council Approved@

# THANK YOU!

114 Bizspace Limited, Business Park, Kings Road, Tyseley, Birmingham, B112AL

PHONE NUMBER:
+44 7878068906

# RECEIPT

RECEIPT

RECEIPT

# PARADISE TRADING LTD (BIRMINGHAM)

Website: www.kulsoomtrading.com

# INVOICE

TO: _____   DATE: _____

_____

| ITEM | QTY | PRICE | TOTAL |
|------|-----|-------|-------|
|      |     |       |       |
|      |     |       |       |
|      |     |       |       |
|      |     |       |       |
|      |     |       |       |

TOTAL

Registered Company of UK & EU.@
Trademarked @
Product tested Certified@
Council Approved@

## THANK YOU!

114 Bizspace Limited, Business Park, Kings Road, Tyseley, Birmingham, B112AL

PHONE NUMBER:
+44 7878068906

RECEIPT

RECEIPT

RECEIPT

# INVOICE

TO: _____

_____

DATE: _____

| ITEM | QTY | PRICE | TOTAL |
|------|-----|-------|-------|
|  |  |  |  |
|  |  |  |  |
|  |  |  |  |
|  |  |  |  |
|  |  |  |  |
|  |  |  |  |

TOTAL

Registered Company of UK & EU.@
Trademarked @
Product tested Certified@
Council Approved@

## THANK YOU!

114 Bizspace Limited, Business Park, Kings Road, Tyseley, Birmingham, B112AL

PHONE NUMBER:
+44 7878068906

RECEIPT

RECEIPT

RECEIPT

# PARADISE TRADING LTD (BIRMINGHAM)

## Website: www.kulsoomtrading.com

# INVOICE

TO: _____     DATE: _____

_____

| ITEM | QTY | PRICE | TOTAL |
| --- | --- | --- | --- |
| | | | |
| | | | |
| | | | |
| | | | |
| | | | |

TOTAL

Registered Company of UK & EU.@
Trademarked @
Product tested Certified@
Council Approved@

## THANK YOU!

114 Bizspace Limited, Business Park, Kings Road, Tyseley, Birmingham, B112AL

PHONE NUMBER:
+44 7878068906

RECEIPT

RECEIPT

RECEIPT

# PARADISE TRADING LTD (BIRMINGHAM)

Website: www.kulsoomtrading.com

# INVOICE

TO: _____

_____

DATE: _____

| ITEM | QTY | PRICE | TOTAL |
|------|-----|-------|-------|
|  |  |  |  |
|  |  |  |  |
|  |  |  |  |
|  |  |  |  |
|  |  |  |  |
|  |  |  |  |

TOTAL

Registered Company of UK & EU.@
Trademarked @
Product tested Certified@
Council Approved@

# THANK YOU!

114 Bizspace Limited, Business Park, Kings Road, Tyseley, Birmingham, B112AL

PHONE NUMBER:
+44 7878068906

**RECEIPT**

RECEIPT

RECEIPT

# PARADISE TRADING LTD (BIRMINGHAM)

Website: www.kulsoomtrading.com

# INVOICE

TO: _____     DATE: _____

_____

| ITEM | QTY | PRICE | TOTAL |
|------|-----|-------|-------|
|      |     |       |       |
|      |     |       |       |
|      |     |       |       |
|      |     |       |       |
|      |     |       |       |
|      |     |       |       |
|      |     |       |       |

TOTAL

Registered Company of UK & EU.@
Trademarked @
Product tested Certified@
Council Approved@

## THANK YOU!

114 Bizspace Limited, Business Park, Kings Road, Tyseley, Birmingham, B112AL

PHONE NUMBER:
+44 7878068906

RECEIPT

RECEIPT

RECEIPT

# PARADISE TRADING LTD (BIRMINGHAM)

## Website: www.kulsoomtrading.com

# INVOICE

TO: _____     DATE: _____

_____

| ITEM | QTY | PRICE | TOTAL |
|---|---|---|---|
| | | | |
| | | | |
| | | | |
| | | | |
| | | | |
| | | | |
| | | | |

**TOTAL**

Registered Company of UK & EU.@
Trademarked @
Product tested Certified@
Council Approved@

# THANK YOU!

114 Bizspace Limited, Business Park, Kings Road, Tyseley, Birmingham, B112AL

PHONE NUMBER:
+44 7878068906

RECEIPT

RECEIPT

# RECEIPT

# INVOICE

TO: _____     DATE: _____

_____

| ITEM | QTY | PRICE | TOTAL |
|------|-----|-------|-------|
|      |     |       |       |
|      |     |       |       |
|      |     |       |       |
|      |     |       |       |
|      |     |       |       |
|      |     |       |       |

TOTAL

**THANK YOU!**

114 Bizspace Limited, Business Park, Kings Road, Tyseley, Birmingham, B112AL

PHONE NUMBER:
+44 7878068906

RECEIPT

# RECEIPT

RECEIPT

# INVOICE

TO: _____   DATE: _____

_____

| ITEM | QTY | PRICE | TOTAL |
|------|-----|-------|-------|
|  |  |  |  |
|  |  |  |  |
|  |  |  |  |
|  |  |  |  |
|  |  |  |  |
|  |  |  |  |

**TOTAL**

## THANK YOU!

114 Bizspace Limited, Business Park, Kings Road, Tyseley, Birmingham, B112AL

PHONE NUMBER:
+44 7878068906

RECEIPT

# RECEIPT

RECEIPT

# INVOICE

TO: _____    DATE: _____

_____

| ITEM | QTY | PRICE | TOTAL |
|------|-----|-------|-------|
|      |     |       |       |
|      |     |       |       |
|      |     |       |       |
|      |     |       |       |
|      |     |       |       |

**TOTAL**

Registered Company of UK & EU.@
Trademarked @
Product tested Certified@
Council Approved@

**THANK YOU!**

114 Bizspace Limited, Business Park, Kings Road, Tyseley, Birmingham, B112AL

PHONE NUMBER:
+44 7878068906

RECEIPT

RECEIPT

RECEIPT

# PARADISE TRADING LTD (BIRMINGHAM)

Website: www.kulsoomtrading.com

# INVOICE

TO: _____        DATE: _____

_____

| ITEM | QTY | PRICE | TOTAL |
|------|-----|-------|-------|
|  |  |  |  |
|  |  |  |  |
|  |  |  |  |
|  |  |  |  |
|  |  |  |  |

TOTAL

Registered Company of UK & EU.@
Trademarked @
Product tested Certified@
Council Approved@

**THANK YOU!**

114 Bizspace Limited, Business Park, Kings Road, Tyseley, Birmingham, B112AL

PHONE NUMBER:
+44 7878068906

RECEIPT

RECEIPT

RECEIPT

# PARADISE TRADING LTD (BIRMINGHAM)

Website: www.kulsoomtrading.com

# INVOICE

TO: _____     DATE: _____

_____

| ITEM | QTY | PRICE | TOTAL |
|------|-----|-------|-------|
|  |  |  |  |
|  |  |  |  |
|  |  |  |  |
|  |  |  |  |

TOTAL

Registered Company of UK & EU.@
Trademarked @
Product tested Certified@
Council Approved@

# THANK YOU!

114 Bizspace Limited, Business Park, Kings Road, Tyseley, Birmingham, B112AL

PHONE NUMBER:
+44 7878068906

RECEIPT

RECEIPT

RECEIPT

# INVOICE

TO: _____   DATE: _____

_____

| ITEM | QTY | PRICE | TOTAL |
|------|-----|-------|-------|
|      |     |       |       |
|      |     |       |       |
|      |     |       |       |
|      |     |       |       |
|      |     |       |       |
|      |     |       |       |

TOTAL

Registered Company of UK & EU.@
Trademarked @
Product tested Certified@
Council Approved@

**THANK YOU!**

114 Bizspace Limited, Business Park, Kings Road, Tyseley, Birmingham, B112AL

PHONE NUMBER:
+44 7878068906

RECEIPT

# RECEIPT

# RECEIPT

# INVOICE

TO: _____          DATE: _____

_____

| ITEM | QTY | PRICE | TOTAL |
|------|-----|-------|-------|
|      |     |       |       |
|      |     |       |       |
|      |     |       |       |
|      |     |       |       |
|      |     |       |       |

TOTAL

Registered Company of UK & EU.@
Trademarked @
Product tested Certified@
Council Approved@

## THANK YOU!

114 Bizspace Limited, Business Park, Kings Road, Tyseley, Birmingham, B112AL

PHONE NUMBER:
+44 7878068906

# RECEIPT

RECEIPT

RECEIPT

# PARADISE TRADING LTD (BIRMINGHAM)

Website: www.kulsoomtrading.com

# INVOICE

TO: _____    DATE: _____

_____

| ITEM | QTY | PRICE | TOTAL |
|------|-----|-------|-------|
|      |     |       |       |
|      |     |       |       |
|      |     |       |       |
|      |     |       |       |
|      |     |       |       |
|      |     |       |       |
|      |     |       |       |

TOTAL

**THANK YOU!**

114 Bizspace Limited, Business Park, Kings Road, Tyseley, Birmingham, B112AL

PHONE NUMBER:
+44 7878068906

RECEIPT

# RECEIPT

# RECEIPT

# PARADISE TRADING LTD (BIRMINGHAM)

Website: www.kulsoomtrading.com

# INVOICE

TO: _____        DATE: _____

_____

| ITEM | QTY | PRICE | TOTAL |
|------|-----|-------|-------|
|      |     |       |       |
|      |     |       |       |
|      |     |       |       |
|      |     |       |       |
|      |     |       |       |
|      |     |       |       |

TOTAL

**THANK YOU!**

114 Bizspace Limited, Business Park, Kings Road, Tyseley, Birmingham, B112AL

PHONE NUMBER:
+44 7878068906

RECEIPT

RECEIPT

RECEIPT

# INVOICE

TO: _____  DATE: _____

_____

| ITEM | QTY | PRICE | TOTAL |
|------|-----|-------|-------|
|      |     |       |       |
|      |     |       |       |
|      |     |       |       |
|      |     |       |       |
|      |     |       |       |
|      |     |       |       |

TOTAL

Registered Company of UK & EU.@
Trademarked @
Product tested Certified@
Council Approved@

**THANK YOU!**

114 Bizspace Limited, Business Park, Kings Road, Tyseley, Birmingham, B112AL

PHONE NUMBER:
+44 7878068906

# RECEIPT

RECEIPT

RECEIPT

# INVOICE

TO: _____     DATE: _____

_____

| ITEM | QTY | PRICE | TOTAL |
|------|-----|-------|-------|
|      |     |       |       |
|      |     |       |       |
|      |     |       |       |
|      |     |       |       |
|      |     |       |       |
|      |     |       |       |

TOTAL

Registered Company of UK & EU.@
Trademarked @
Product tested Certified@
Council Approved@

## THANK YOU!

114 Bizspace Limited, Business Park, Kings Road, Tyseley, Birmingham, B112AL

PHONE NUMBER:
+44 7878068906

RECEIPT

RECEIPT

RECEIPT

# INVOICE

TO: _____     DATE: _____

_____

| ITEM | QTY | PRICE | TOTAL |
|------|-----|-------|-------|
|      |     |       |       |
|      |     |       |       |
|      |     |       |       |
|      |     |       |       |
|      |     |       |       |
|      |     |       |       |
|      |     |       |       |

TOTAL

Registered Company of UK & EU.@
Trademarked @
Product tested Certified@
Council Approved@

## THANK YOU!

114 Bizspace Limited, Business Park, Kings Road, Tyseley, Birmingham, B112AL

PHONE NUMBER:
+44 7878068906

# RECEIPT

RECEIPT

RECEIPT

# PARADISE TRADING LTD (BIRMINGHAM)

## Website: www.kulsoomtrading.com

# INVOICE

TO: _____     DATE: _____

_____

| ITEM | QTY | PRICE | TOTAL |
|------|-----|-------|-------|
|      |     |       |       |
|      |     |       |       |
|      |     |       |       |
|      |     |       |       |
|      |     |       |       |
|      |     |       |       |
|      |     |       |       |

TOTAL

Registered Company of UK & EU.@
Trademarked @
Product tested Certified@
Council Approved@

# THANK YOU!

114 Bizspace Limited, Business Park, Kings Road, Tyseley, Birmingham, B112AL

PHONE NUMBER:
+44 7878068906

RECEIPT

# RECEIPT

RECEIPT

# PARADISE TRADING LTD (BIRMINGHAM)

Website: www.kulsoomtrading.com

# INVOICE

TO: _____     DATE: _____

_____

| ITEM | QTY | PRICE | TOTAL |
|------|-----|-------|-------|
|      |     |       |       |
|      |     |       |       |
|      |     |       |       |
|      |     |       |       |
|      |     |       |       |

TOTAL

Registered Company of UK & EU.@
Trademarked @
Product tested Certified@
Council Approved@

## THANK YOU!

114 Bizspace Limited, Business Park, Kings Road, Tyseley, Birmingham, B112AL

PHONE NUMBER:
+44 7878068906

# RECEIPT

RECEIPT

**RECEIPT**

# PARADISE TRADING LTD (BIRMINGHAM)

Website: www.kulsoomtrading.com

# INVOICE

TO: _____     DATE: _____

_____

| ITEM | QTY | PRICE | TOTAL |
|------|-----|-------|-------|
|      |     |       |       |
|      |     |       |       |
|      |     |       |       |
|      |     |       |       |
|      |     |       |       |
|      |     |       |       |
|      |     |       |       |

TOTAL

Registered Company of UK & EU.@
Trademarked @
Product tested Certified@
Council Approved@

## THANK YOU!

114 Bizspace Limited, Business Park, Kings Road, Tyseley, Birmingham, B112AL

PHONE NUMBER:
+44 7878068906

RECEIPT

# RECEIPT

# RECEIPT

# PARADISE TRADING LTD (BIRMINGHAM)

Website: www.kulsoomtrading.com

# INVOICE

TO: _____    DATE: _____

_____

| ITEM | QTY | PRICE | TOTAL |
|------|-----|-------|-------|
|      |     |       |       |
|      |     |       |       |
|      |     |       |       |
|      |     |       |       |
|      |     |       |       |
|      |     |       |       |
|      |     |       |       |

TOTAL

Registered Company of UK & EU.@
Trademarked @
Product tested Certified@
Council Approved@

## THANK YOU!

114 Bizspace Limited, Business Park, Kings Road, Tyseley, Birmingham, B112AL

PHONE NUMBER:
+44 7878068906

RECEIPT

RECEIPT

**RECEIPT**

# PARADISE TRADING LTD (BIRMINGHAM)

Website: www.kulsoomtrading.com

# INVOICE

TO: _____

_____

DATE: _____

| ITEM | QTY | PRICE | TOTAL |
|------|-----|-------|-------|
|      |     |       |       |
|      |     |       |       |
|      |     |       |       |
|      |     |       |       |
|      |     |       |       |
|      |     |       |       |

TOTAL

## THANK YOU!

114 Bizspace Limited, Business Park, Kings Road, Tyseley, Birmingham, B112AL

PHONE NUMBER:
+44 7878068906

RECEIPT

# RECEIPT

# RECEIPT

# PARADISE TRADING LTD (BIRMINGHAM)

Website: www.kulsoomtrading.com

# INVOICE

TO: _____     DATE: _____

_____

| ITEM | QTY | PRICE | TOTAL |
|------|-----|-------|-------|
|      |     |       |       |
|      |     |       |       |
|      |     |       |       |
|      |     |       |       |
|      |     |       |       |
|      |     |       |       |

TOTAL

Registered Company of UK & EU.@
Trademarked @
Product tested Certified@
Council Approved@

## THANK YOU!

114 Bizspace Limited, Business Park, Kings Road, Tyseley, Birmingham, B112AL

PHONE NUMBER:
+44 7878068906

# RECEIPT

RECEIPT

# RECEIPT

# PARADISE TRADING LTD (BIRMINGHAM)

Website: www.kulsoomtrading.com

# INVOICE

TO: _____        DATE: _____

_____

| ITEM | QTY | PRICE | TOTAL |
|------|-----|-------|-------|
|  |  |  |  |
|  |  |  |  |
|  |  |  |  |
|  |  |  |  |
|  |  |  |  |
|  |  |  |  |

TOTAL

Registered Company of UK & EU.@
Trademarked @
Product tested Certified@
Council Approved@

# THANK YOU!

114 Bizspace Limited, Business Park, Kings Road, Tyseley, Birmingham, B112AL

PHONE NUMBER:
+44 7878068906

RECEIPT

RECEIPT

# RECEIPT

# PARADISE TRADING LTD (BIRMINGHAM)

Website: www.kulsoomtrading.com

# INVOICE

TO: _____   DATE: _____

_____

| ITEM | QTY | PRICE | TOTAL |
|------|-----|-------|-------|
|  |  |  |  |
|  |  |  |  |
|  |  |  |  |
|  |  |  |  |
|  |  |  |  |
|  |  |  |  |

TOTAL

Registered Company of UK & EU.@
Trademarked @
Product tested Certified@
Council Approved@

# THANK YOU!

114 Bizspace Limited, Business Park, Kings Road, Tyseley, Birmingham, B112AL

PHONE NUMBER:
+44 7878068906

RECEIPT

RECEIPT

RECEIPT

# PARADISE TRADING LTD (BIRMINGHAM)

## Website: www.kulsoomtrading.com

# INVOICE

TO: _____ DATE: _____

_____

| ITEM | QTY | PRICE | TOTAL |
|------|-----|-------|-------|
|      |     |       |       |
|      |     |       |       |
|      |     |       |       |
|      |     |       |       |
|      |     |       |       |

TOTAL

# THANK YOU!

114 Bizspace Limited, Business Park, Kings Road, Tyseley, Birmingham, B112AL

PHONE NUMBER:
+44 7878068906

RECEIPT

RECEIPT

# RECEIPT

# INVOICE

TO: _____    DATE: _____

_____

| ITEM | QTY | PRICE | TOTAL |
|------|-----|-------|-------|
|      |     |       |       |
|      |     |       |       |
|      |     |       |       |
|      |     |       |       |
|      |     |       |       |
|      |     |       |       |

TOTAL

Registered Company of UK & EU.@
Trademarked @
Product tested Certified@
Council Approved@

## THANK YOU!

114 Bizspace Limited, Business Park, Kings Road, Tyseley, Birmingham, B112AL

PHONE NUMBER:
+44 7878068906

RECEIPT

RECEIPT

RECEIPT

# INVOICE

TO: _____        DATE: _____

_____

| ITEM | QTY | PRICE | TOTAL |
|------|-----|-------|-------|
|      |     |       |       |
|      |     |       |       |
|      |     |       |       |
|      |     |       |       |
|      |     |       |       |

TOTAL

Registered Company of UK & EU.@
Trademarked @
Product tested Certified@
Council Approved@

## THANK YOU!

114 Bizspace Limited, Business Park, Kings Road, Tyseley, Birmingham, B112AL

PHONE NUMBER:
+44 7878068906

RECEIPT

RECEIPT

RECEIPT

# INVOICE

TO: _____  DATE: _____

_____

| ITEM | QTY | PRICE | TOTAL |
|------|-----|-------|-------|
|      |     |       |       |
|      |     |       |       |
|      |     |       |       |
|      |     |       |       |
|      |     |       |       |
|      |     |       |       |

TOTAL

Registered Company of UK & EU.@
Trademarked @
Product tested Certified@
Council Approved@

**THANK YOU!**

114 Bizspace Limited, Business Park, Kings Road, Tyseley, Birmingham, B112AL

PHONE NUMBER:
+44 7878068906

# RECEIPT

RECEIPT

RECEIPT

# PARADISE TRADING LTD (BIRMINGHAM)

## Website: www.kulsoomtrading.com

# INVOICE

TO: _____     DATE: _____

_____

| ITEM | QTY | PRICE | TOTAL |
|------|-----|-------|-------|
|      |     |       |       |
|      |     |       |       |
|      |     |       |       |
|      |     |       |       |
|      |     |       |       |
|      |     |       |       |

TOTAL

Registered Company of UK & EU.@
Trademarked @
Product tested Certified@
Council Approved@

# THANK YOU!

114 Bizspace Limited, Business Park, Kings Road, Tyseley, Birmingham, B112AL

PHONE NUMBER:
+44 7878068906

RECEIPT

RECEIPT

RECEIPT

# INVOICE

TO: _____    DATE: _____

_____

| ITEM | QTY | PRICE | TOTAL |
|------|-----|-------|-------|
|      |     |       |       |
|      |     |       |       |
|      |     |       |       |
|      |     |       |       |
|      |     |       |       |

TOTAL

# THANK YOU!

# RECEIPT

RECEIPT

RECEIPT

# PARADISE TRADING LTD (BIRMINGHAM)

Website: www.kulsoomtrading.com

# INVOICE

TO: _____    DATE: _____

_____

| ITEM | QTY | PRICE | TOTAL |
|------|-----|-------|-------|
|      |     |       |       |
|      |     |       |       |
|      |     |       |       |
|      |     |       |       |
|      |     |       |       |
|      |     |       |       |

TOTAL

Registered Company of UK & EU.@
Trademarked @
Product tested Certified@
Council Approved@

## THANK YOU!

114 Bizspace Limited, Business Park, Kings Road, Tyseley, Birmingham, B112AL

PHONE NUMBER:
+44 7878068906

RECEIPT

RECEIPT

# RECEIPT

# PARADISE TRADING LTD (BIRMINGHAM)

Website: www.kulsoomtrading.com

# INVOICE

TO: _____       DATE: _____

_____

| ITEM | QTY | PRICE | TOTAL |
|------|-----|-------|-------|
|  |  |  |  |
|  |  |  |  |
|  |  |  |  |
|  |  |  |  |
|  |  |  |  |

TOTAL

Registered Company of UK & EU.@
Trademarked @
Product tested Certified@
Council Approved@

# THANK YOU!

114 Bizspace Limited, Business Park, Kings Road, Tyseley, Birmingham, B112AL

PHONE NUMBER:
+44 7878068906

RECEIPT

# RECEIPT

RECEIPT

# PARADISE TRADING LTD (BIRMINGHAM)

## Website: www.kulsoomtrading.com

# INVOICE

TO: _____   DATE: _____

_____

| ITEM | QTY | PRICE | TOTAL |
|------|-----|-------|-------|
|      |     |       |       |
|      |     |       |       |
|      |     |       |       |
|      |     |       |       |
|      |     |       |       |
|      |     |       |       |
|      |     |       |       |

TOTAL

Registered Company of UK & EU.@
Trademarked @
Product tested Certified@
Council Approved@

# THANK YOU!

114 Bizspace Limited, Business Park, Kings Road, Tyseley, Birmingham, B112AL

PHONE NUMBER:
+44 7878068906

RECEIPT

RECEIPT

RECEIPT

# PARADISE TRADING LTD (BIRMINGHAM)

Website: www.kulsoomtrading.com

# INVOICE

TO: _____     DATE: _____

_____

| ITEM | QTY | PRICE | TOTAL |
|------|-----|-------|-------|
|      |     |       |       |
|      |     |       |       |
|      |     |       |       |
|      |     |       |       |
|      |     |       |       |
|      |     |       |       |

TOTAL

Registered Company of UK & EU.@
Trademarked @
Product tested Certified@
Council Approved@

# THANK YOU!

114 Bizspace Limited, Business Park, Kings Road, Tyseley, Birmingham, B112AL

PHONE NUMBER:
+44 7878068906

RECEIPT

RECEIPT

RECEIPT

# PARADISE TRADING LTD (BIRMINGHAM)

Website: www.kulsoomtrading.com

# INVOICE

TO: _____   DATE: _____

_____

| ITEM | QTY | PRICE | TOTAL |
|------|-----|-------|-------|
|  |  |  |  |

TOTAL

**THANK YOU!**

114 Bizspace Limited, Business Park, Kings Road, Tyseley, Birmingham, B112AL

PHONE NUMBER:
+44 7878068906

RECEIPT

RECEIPT

# RECEIPT

# PARADISE TRADING     LTD
## (BIRMINGHAM)
Website: www.kulsoomtrading.com

# INVOICE

TO: _____  DATE: _____

_____

| ITEM | QTY | PRICE | TOTAL |
|------|-----|-------|-------|
|  |  |  |  |
|  |  |  |  |
|  |  |  |  |
|  |  |  |  |
|  |  |  |  |
|  |  |  |  |
|  |  |  |  |

TOTAL

Registered Company of UK & EU.@
Trademarked @
Product tested Certified@
Council Approved@

**THANK YOU!**

114 Bizspace Limited, Business Park, Kings Road, Tyseley, Birmingham, B112AL

PHONE NUMBER:
+44 7878068906

RECEIPT

RECEIPT

# RECEIPT

# PARADISE TRADING LTD (BIRMINGHAM)

Website: www.kulsoomtrading.com

# INVOICE

TO: _____      DATE: _____

_____

| ITEM | QTY | PRICE | TOTAL |
|------|-----|-------|-------|
|  |  |  |  |
|  |  |  |  |
|  |  |  |  |
|  |  |  |  |
|  |  |  |  |
|  |  |  |  |
|  |  |  |  |

TOTAL

Registered Company of UK & EU.@
Trademarked @
Product tested Certified@
Council Approved@

114 Bizspace Limited, Business Park, Kings Road, Tyseley, Birmingham, B112AL

THANK YOU!

PHONE NUMBER:
+44 7878068906

RECEIPT

# RECEIPT

**RECEIPT**

# PARADISE TRADING LTD (BIRMINGHAM)

## Website: www.kulsoomtrading.com

# INVOICE

TO: _____      DATE: _____

_____

| ITEM | QTY | PRICE | TOTAL |
|------|-----|-------|-------|
|      |     |       |       |
|      |     |       |       |
|      |     |       |       |
|      |     |       |       |
|      |     |       |       |
|      |     |       |       |

TOTAL

Registered Company of UK & EU.@
Trademarked @
Product tested Certified@
Council Approved@

# THANK YOU!

114 Bizspace Limited, Business Park, Kings Road, Tyseley, Birmingham, B112AL

PHONE NUMBER:
+44 7878068906

RECEIPT

RECEIPT

RECEIPT

# PARADISE TRADING LTD (BIRMINGHAM)

Website: www.kulsoomtrading.com

# INVOICE

TO: _____     DATE: _____

_____

| ITEM | QTY | PRICE | TOTAL |
|------|-----|-------|-------|
|  |  |  |  |
|  |  |  |  |
|  |  |  |  |
|  |  |  |  |
|  |  |  |  |

TOTAL

Registered Company of UK & EU.@
Trademarked @
Product tested Certified@
Council Approved@

## THANK YOU!

114 Bizspace Limited, Business Park, Kings Road, Tyseley, Birmingham, B112AL

PHONE NUMBER:
+44 7878068906

RECEIPT

RECEIPT

RECEIPT

# PARADISE TRADING LTD (BIRMINGHAM)

Website: www.kulsoomtrading.com

# INVOICE

TO: _____       DATE: _____

_____

| ITEM | QTY | PRICE | TOTAL |
|------|-----|-------|-------|
|      |     |       |       |
|      |     |       |       |
|      |     |       |       |
|      |     |       |       |
|      |     |       |       |
|      |     |       |       |

TOTAL

Registered Company of UK & EU.@
Trademarked @
Product tested Certified@
Council Approved@

## THANK YOU!

114 Bizspace Limited, Business Park, Kings Road, Tyseley, Birmingham, B112AL

PHONE NUMBER:
+44 7878068906

RECEIPT

RECEIPT

RECEIPT

# INVOICE

TO: _____     DATE: _____

_____

| ITEM | QTY | PRICE | TOTAL |
|------|-----|-------|-------|
|      |     |       |       |
|      |     |       |       |
|      |     |       |       |
|      |     |       |       |
|      |     |       |       |
|      |     |       |       |

TOTAL

Registered Company of UK & EU.@
Trademarked @
Product tested Certified@
Council Approved@

**THANK YOU!**

114 Bizspace Limited, Business Park, Kings Road, Tyseley, Birmingham, B112AL

PHONE NUMBER:
+44 7878068906

RECEIPT

RECEIPT

RECEIPT

# INVOICE

TO: _____      DATE: _____

_____

| ITEM | QTY | PRICE | TOTAL |
|------|-----|-------|-------|
|      |     |       |       |
|      |     |       |       |
|      |     |       |       |
|      |     |       |       |
|      |     |       |       |
|      |     |       |       |

TOTAL

Registered Company of UK & EU.@
Trademarked @
Product tested Certified@
Council Approved@

## THANK YOU!

114 Bizspace Limited, Business Park, Kings Road, Tyseley, Birmingham, B112AL

PHONE NUMBER:
+44 7878068906

RECEIPT

RECEIPT

RECEIPT

# PARADISE TRADING LTD (BIRMINGHAM)

Website: www.kulsoomtrading.com

# INVOICE

TO: _____      DATE: _____

_____

| ITEM | QTY | PRICE | TOTAL |
|------|-----|-------|-------|
|      |     |       |       |
|      |     |       |       |
|      |     |       |       |
|      |     |       |       |
|      |     |       |       |
|      |     |       |       |
|      |     |       |       |

TOTAL

Registered Company of UK & EU.@
Trademarked @
Product tested Certified@
Council Approved@

**THANK YOU!**

114 Bizspace Limited, Business Park, Kings Road, Tyseley, Birmingham, B112AL

PHONE NUMBER:
+44 7878068906

RECEIPT

RECEIPT

**RECEIPT**

Printed in Great Britain
by Amazon

81253500R00115